Surviving History

THE FRENCH REVOLUTION

Virginia Loh-Hagan

45TH PARALLEL PRESS

Published in the United States of America by Cherry Lake Publishing Group
Ann Arbor, Michigan
www.cherrylakepublishing.com
Reading Adviser: Marla Conn, MS, Ed., Literacy specialist, Read-Ability, Inc.

Book Designer: Melinda Millward

Photo Credits: © Vladiczech/Shutterstock.com, cover, 1; © Morphart Creation/Shutterstock.com, 4; © duncan1890/istockphoto.com, 6, 18, 24, 27; © Cynthia Liang/Shutterstock.com, 8; © Marzolino/Shutterstock.com, 10; © Grafissimo/istockphoto.com, back cover, 12; © Apichon Chaochon/Shutterstock.com, 14; © andrey_l/Shutterstock.com, 16; © Yavuz Sariyildiz/Shutterstock.com, 20; © whitemay/istockphoto.com, 22; © Ludovic Debono/istockphoto.com, 28

Graphic Element Credits: © Milos Djapovic/Shutterstock.com, back cover, front cover; © cajoer/Shutterstock.com, back cover, front cover, multiple interior pages; © GUSAK OLENA/Shutterstock.com, back cover, multiple interior pages; © Miloje/Shutterstock.com, front cover; © Rtstudio/Shutterstock.com, multiple interior pages; © Konstantin Nikiteev/Dreamstime.com, 29

45TH Parallel Press is an imprint of Cherry Lake Publishing Group.

Library of Congress Cataloging-in-Publication Data

Names: Loh-Hagan, Virginia, author.
Title: The French Revolution / by Virginia Loh-Hagan.
Description: Ann Arbor, Michigan: Cherry Lake Publishing, [2021] | Series: Surviving history | Includes bibliographical references and index.
Identifiers: LCCN 2020003345 (print) | LCCN 2020003346 (ebook) | ISBN 9781534169135 (hardcover) | ISBN 9781534170810 (paperback) | ISBN 9781534172654 (pdf) | ISBN 9781534174498 (ebook)
Subjects: LCSH: France—History—Revolution, 1789-1799—Juvenile literature.
Classification: LCC DC148 .L64 2021 (print) | LCC DC148 (ebook) | DDC 944.04—dc23
LC record available at https://lccn.loc.gov/2020003345
LC ebook record available at https://lccn.loc.gov/2020003346

Printed in the United States of America
Corporate Graphics

TABLE OF CONTENTS

INTRODUCTION

French revolutionaries took down and rebuilt their nation.

The French **Revolution** took place from 1789 to 1799. Revolution means an overthrow. The common people took control of the government. They were called revolutionaries. They overthrew the **monarchy**. Monarchy is a government ruled by a king or queen. At this time, King Louis XVI and Queen Marie Antoinette were the rulers. They were killed in 1793.

Revolutionaries were unhappy. France was in **debt**. Debt means owing money. This caused food shortages. Many of the common people were suffering. They were starving. They resented the monarchy. They wanted a voice in government. So, they rioted. They looted.

The French Revolution brought on new ideas and reforms. Reforms are changes. Many governments today are influenced by the French Revolution.

The French Revolution began on July 14, 1789. Revolutionaries stormed the Bastille. The Bastille was a jail. The French Revolution ended in November 1799. General Napoleon Bonaparte overthrew the revolutionary government. He made himself the leader.

The French Revolution was not a good time for the **noble** class. Nobles were rich. The Revolution changed France. It ended the French monarchy. It ended the French social class system. It took power away from the Catholic church.

The French Revolution also changed the world. Monarchies lost power. Governments led by the people became popular. Women were granted more rights. **Slavery** was questioned. Slavery is a system in which people are forced to work without pay.

FAIR OR UNFAIR?

France's system of 3 estates is called the old regime.

The French were divided into 3 social groups. These groups were called **estates**. The first estate included church leaders. The second estate included nobles. The third estate included the common people. The king and queen were a separate group. They ruled over all.

This system was unfair. The first and second estates had the most power. The third estate had the most people. But they had little power. They were blocked from positions of power.

The monarch and nobles taxed the third estate. They got most of their money from land taxes. This upset the common people.

QUESTION 1

Which estate would you have been?

A You were third estate. You owned small farms. Or you were a worker. You worked for the first and second estates. You lived in the city or country. You had the least of the 3 estates. You paid the most taxes. You were mad.

B You were first estate. You were **clergy**. Clergy means church leaders. You didn't pay taxes. You taxed the second and third estates.

C You were second estate. You were a soldier or politician. You didn't have to do community service. You owned most of the land. You were lightly taxed. You lived a fancy life. You bought expensive things. You didn't want change.

The king tried to stop the revolution. He created an Estates-General. This was a group with members from all 3 social groups.

SURVIVOR BIOGRAPHY

Jeanne-Marie Roland was better known as Madame Roland. She lived from 1754 to 1793. Her husband was elected to office. Roland directed her husband's career. She made many connections. She met politicians. She met journalists. She published reports about the revolution. She lived in Paris. She was famous for hosting salons. Salons are social meetings. They were the meeting place for the Girondins. This group fought against the monarchy. Roland became their leader. She was smart. She started reading at age 4. She was good at making deals. In June 1793, she was the first Girondin to be arrested during the Reign of Terror. While in jail, she wrote about her life. Her writing is important. It gives a lot of information about the French Revolution. Roland was killed by the **guillotine** on November 8, 1793. Guillotines are machines. They quickly chop off people's heads. Before she died, she said, "O Liberty. What crimes are committed in thy name!"

BREAD OR BRAWL?

There was a **rise in population**. This meant there were more people than food.

There was a bad winter in 1788. No crops grew. This caused **famine**. Famine is a lack of food. Bread was in short supply. This raised the costs of bread. Not having enough food enraged the third estate.

Revolutionaries stormed the Bastille. They wanted guns. They wanted grains to make bread. For weeks, they **protested**. Protest is to fight for change. Revolutionaries demanded cheaper bread. They rioted. Some of these riots were violent.

Baguettes may have been created during the French Revolution. Baguettes are long, narrow loaves. They're called "equality breads." All estates ate them. Baguettes used an untaxed type of flour. Bakers sold baguettes to **evade** taxes. Evade means to skip.

QUESTION 2

What type of bread would you have eaten?

A You ate cheap bread. You ate **boules**. Boules are bread balls. You ate **maslin**. Maslin bread is a mix of wheat and rye.

B You were a farmer. You raised your own food. You had your own grain. You made your own bread.

C You were rich. You hired soldiers to protect your grain supplies. You ate light, flaky bread loaves. You ate **manchet**. Manchet is white bread. It's refined wheat. It's high quality. It takes time to make.

The king's job was to feed the people. He was called the baker of the kingdom.

SURVIVAL BY THE NUMBERS

- The Reign of Terror killed around 27,000 people. About 17,000 were executed. About 10,000 died in jail.
- Between September 1793 and July 1794, about 200,000 French men and women were arrested. This is about 1 in 50 French people.
- Vendée was a small province in France. In 1794, a revolt broke out. About 170,000 people died.
- There was a battle at Nantes from 1793 to 1794. People were drowned. Between 1,800 and 4,000 people died in drownings.
- The September Massacres of 1792 were bloody. They took place over 3 days. Mobs killed over 1,200 people.
- There were over 652 food riots from 1760 to 1789.
- Before the French Revolution, there were about 26 million French people. About 400,000 were nobles. After the revolution, there were only 15,000 nobles left.

TERROR OR DEATH?

Guillotine killings became a show. People came to watch.

Maximilien de Robespierre led the **Jacobins**. Jacobins were extreme revolutionaries. They believed violence was needed to establish order. Robespierre commanded the Reign of Terror. This reign lasted from 1793 to 1794.

The Jacobins stamped out their enemies. They arrested and killed people accused of **treason**. Treason is disloyalty. The Jacobins created a new calendar. They banned Christianity. They killed many people with the guillotine.

Robespierre had a list of disloyal people to kill. This angered people. Robespierre became dangerous. He was guillotined in July 1794. This ended the Reign of Terror.

QUESTION 3

What would be your risks of being guillotined during the Reign of Terror?

A You were a Jacobin. You took charge of the revolutionary government. You wanted to protect the revolution's goals. You wanted to keep the revolution going.

B You were a Girondin. Girondins were moderate revolutionaries. They owned businesses. They were educated. They supported the revolution. But they didn't support the Jacobins' violence. Jacobins killed revolutionaries who disagreed with them.

C You were a noble, clergy, or **hoarder**. Hoarders are people who store supplies and don't share. These people were enemies of the revolution.

Robespierre created a new religion called the Cult of the Supreme Being.

SURVIVAL TOOLS

Marie Antoinette, queen of France, only drank water. But she couldn't drink water from the Seine River. This water made her sick. About 3 million people lived in Paris. Their trash and sewage ended up in the Seine. Somtimes, dead bodies were thrown into the Seine. The water was dirty. It had germs. It could cause sicknesses. It could cause death. So, Marie Antoinette got special water. Her water came from natural springs. Her favorite spring was Ville d'Avray. It was near Versailles. Versailles was the royal palace. When Marie Antoinette was in jail, she still got water from Ville d'Avray. She liked to dip biscuits in her water. She also put orange blossoms in her water. Having safe water ensured survival.

JAIL OR FREEDOM?

Some women were arrested for sending money to their families abroad.

Many people were arrested during the Reign of Terror. They were accused of being disloyal. They were disliked. Some people didn't deserve to be jailed. There was no proof. They were just on the wrong side. People were taken to jail. Their names were recorded in books. They were questioned. They were sent to their **cells**. Cells are jail rooms. People were in jail for several weeks or months. They waited to go to court. They waited to be killed.

There were more prisoners than jails. New jails had to be created. Old buildings were turned into jails. Even schools were used as jails.

QUESTION 4

What type of jail cell would you have had?

A You were poor. You were dumped into cramped areas. You shared a cell with others. You were kept in a **dungeon**. Dungeons are underground rooms. They're damp. They have rats.

B You had some money. You used your money to improve your cell. You sent for your things.

C You were rich. You had your own cell. Your cell was aboveground. It had a window with bars. But it was affected by the weather. This means it was often too cold or hot.

King Louis jailed nobles and clergy at the Bastille.

SURVIVAL TIPS

Follow these tips to survive **tuberculosis** (TB). TB is a common lung sickness.

- Get tested. There are different TB tests. There's a skin test. There's a blood test. There's an x-ray.
- Cover mouth when coughing or sneezing. Use a tissue. Put tissue in a closed bag. Throw away bag.
- Wash hands after coughing or sneezing.
- Avoid people who are coughing.
- Take medicine. Follow doctor's orders. It takes 6 to 12 months to kill all TB germs.
- Avoid close contact with people. Don't go to work or school. Stay away from public places.
- Air out your room. Do this often. Open windows. Use fans. Don't let TB germs stay in the room to infect others. Let fresh air move around.
- Avoid areas with TB outbreaks.
- Don't do drugs or drink alcohol. Doing so increases your risk of TB.
- Don't share food or drink with others.

SICK OR HEALTHY?

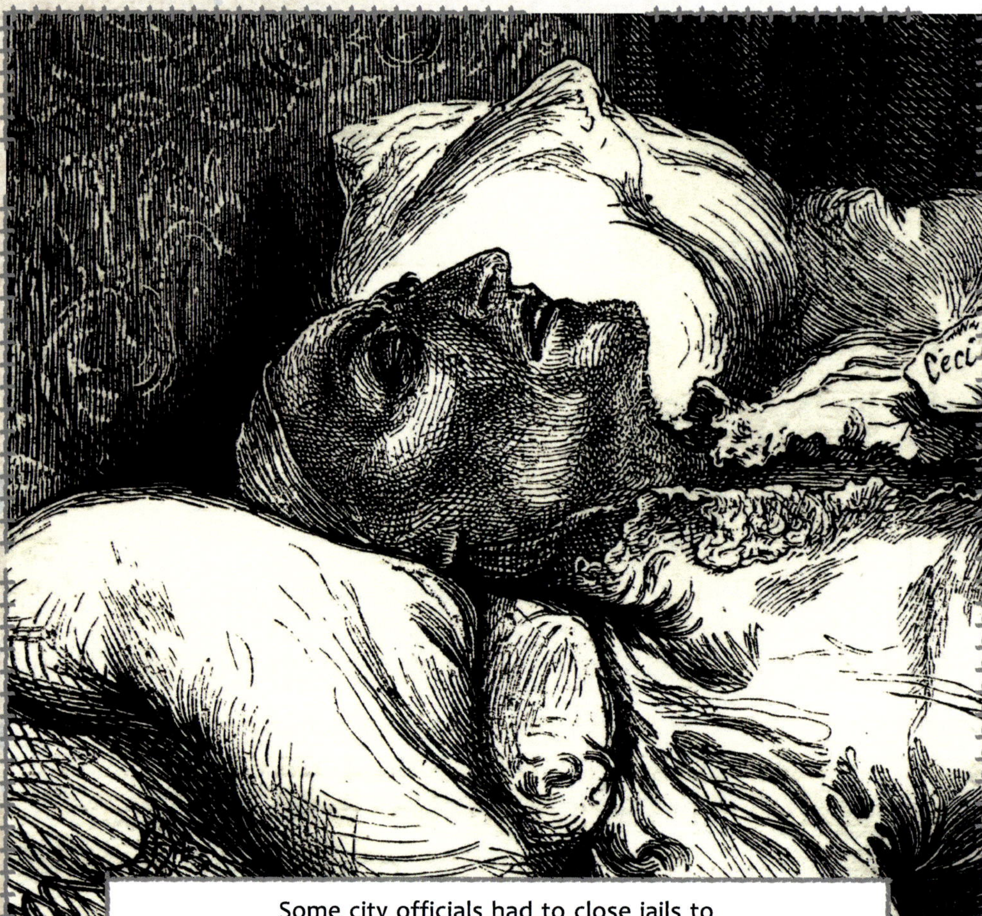

Some city officials had to close jails to stop the spread of sicknesses.

Wars and jails spread sicknesses. People are crammed together. They live in dirty areas. They don't eat well. Their water isn't safe. Their bathrooms are dirty. They don't have access to doctors. They don't have access to medicines.

During the French Revolution, many people died from sicknesses. A common sickness was tuberculosis, or TB. TB is spread through the air. It attacks the lungs. The king's son died of TB. Another common sickness was **typhus**. Typhus causes fevers and rashes.

QUESTION 5

You were lucky. You received care from a doctor. What type of doctor would have treated you?

A You received care from a late-revolutionary doctor. They studied sicknesses. They cut open people who died in Paris hospitals. They did this to learn more about the human body.

B You received care from an early-revolutionary doctor. They wanted to get rid of hospitals. They wanted to get rid of medical schools. They thought everyone could be a doctor.

C You received care from a country doctor. They believed the human body was filled with 4 main substances. These substances were called the "4 **humors**." Humors are body juices. The 4 humors are blood, yellow **bile**, black bile, and **phlegm**. Bile is a sour fluid made by the liver. Phlegm is gunk from the lungs.

Before the French Revolution, doctors worked for nobles. After the revolution, doctors worked for their communities.

SURVIVAL RESULTS

The French king couldn't escape. His face was on coins.

Would you have survived?

Find out! Add up your answers to the chapter questions. Did you have more **A**s, **B**s, or **C**s?

- If you had more **A**s, then you're a survivor! Congrats!
- If you had more **B**s, then you're on the edge. With some luck, you might have just made it.
- If you had more **C**s, then you wouldn't have survived.

Are you happy with your results? Did you have a tie?

Sometimes fate is already decided for us. Follow the link below to our webpage. Scroll until you find the series name *Surviving History*. Click download. Print out the template. Follow the directions to create your own paper die. Read the book again. Roll the die to find your new answers. Did your fate change?

https://cherrylakepublishing.com/teaching_guides

DIGGING DEEPER: DID YOU KNOW ...?

The French Revolution was exciting and terrible. It led to great things. But many lives were lost. Surviving history involves many different factors. Dig deeper. Consider some of the facts below.

QUESTION 1:

Which estate would you have been?

- Third estate wore black suits. They wore white ties. They wore simple hats.
- First estate wore red, purple, or gold robes.
- Second estate wore cloaks and vests with gold stitching. They wore hats with feathers.

QUESTION 2:

What type of bread would you have eaten?

- Poor people were more likely to live in crowded cities. Food was scarce.
- Some bread bakers added sawdust, dirt, and hay. They did this to make the bread last longer.
- Wheat cost a lot. Only rich people could afford it.

QUESTION 3:

What would be your risks of being guillotined during the Reign of Terror?

- The guillotine was more humane than hanging, drowning, or burning.
- The guillotine was called the widow. About 88 percent of the guillotine victims were men. After their death, their wives became widows.
- Sometimes, mobs beat victims to death.

QUESTION 4:

What type of jail cell would you have had?

- Jailed people were called by their cell number.
- Men and women were separated.
- Jailed people who behaved could play cards or chess.

QUESTION 5:

What type of doctor would have treated you?

- Some revolutionaries thought doctors were corrupted by the estate system.
- At this time, doctors used science more. They made observations. They did tests.
- Country doctors bled out sick people. They made people throw up.

GLOSSARY

baguettes (bag-ETS) long, narrow loaves of French bread
bile (BILE) sour fluid made by the liver
boules (BOOL) bread shaped in a ball
cells (SELZ) rooms in prison
clergy (KLUR-jee) church leaders
debt (DET) owing money
dungeon (DUHN-juhn) underground room
estates (ih-STATES) French social groups
evade (ih-VADE) to avoid
famine (FAM-in) extreme lack of food
guillotine (GEE-uh-teen) machine used to behead people
hoarder (HORD-ur) person who stores supplies and doesn't share
humors (HYOO-murz) body juices
Jacobins (JAK-uh-binz) extreme revolutionaries who believed violence was needed to establish order
manchet (MAN-chit) white bread of high quality
maslin (MAZ-lin) bread that is mixed with wheat and rye
monarchy (MAH-nur-kee) a government ruled by a king or queen
noble (NOH-buhl) rich, royal person
phlegm (FLEM) gunk from the lungs
protested (PROH-test-tid) fought for change
revolution (rev-uh-LOO-shun) a forcible overthrow of a government
slavery (SLAY-vur-ee) a system in which people are forced to work without pay
treason (TREE-zuhn) disloyalty
tuberculosis (tuh-bur-kyuh-LOH-sis) an airborne lung disease
typhus (TYE-fus) a disease that causes fevers and rashes

LEARN MORE!

- Gregory, Josh. *The French Revolution*. New York, NY: Children's Press, 2014.
- Pipe, Jim, and David Antram (illust.). *You Wouldn't Want to Be an Aristocrat in the French Revolution!* New York, NY: Franklin Watts, 2008.
- Rau, Dana Meachen, and John O'Brien (illust.). *Who Was Marie Antoinette?* New York, NY: Grosset and Dunlap, 2015.

INDEX

ABOUT THE AUTHOR

Dr. Virginia Loh-Hagan is an author, university professor, and former classroom teacher. One of her favorite places is French Canada (Quebec City). She lives in San Diego with her very tall husband and very naughty dogs.